WORLD IN VIEW
PAKISTAN AND BANGLADESH
Nicholas Nugent

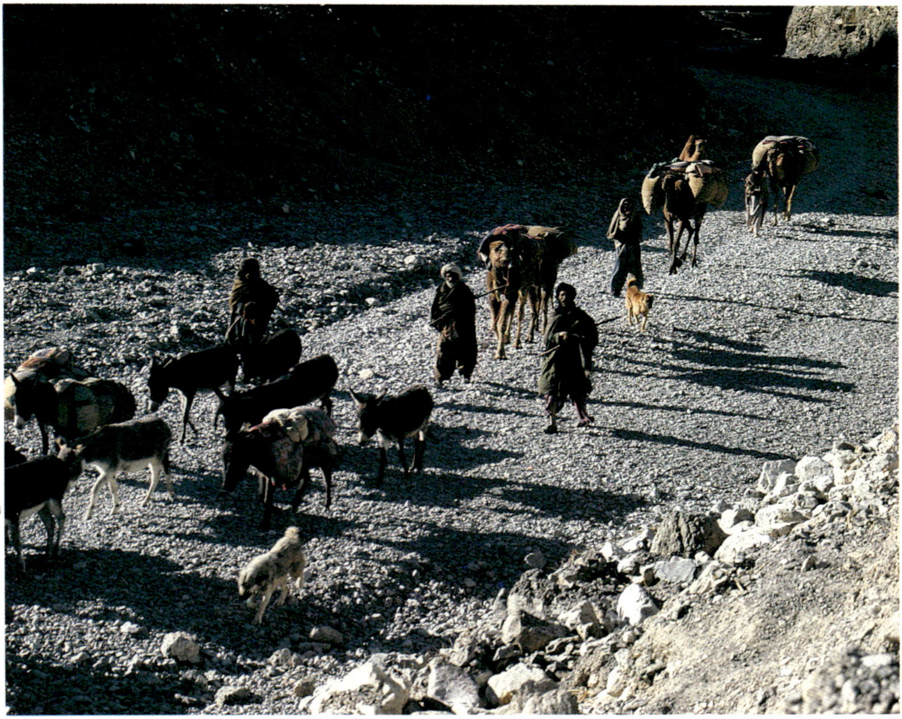

RAINTREE
STECK-VAUGHN
PUBLISHERS
The Steck-Vaughn Company
Austin, Texas

© Copyright 1993, text, Steck-Vaughn Company

All rights reserved. No part of this book may be reproduced or utilized in any form or by any means, electronic or mechanical, including photocopying, recording, or by any information storage and retrieval system, without permission in writing from the Publisher. Inquiries should be addressed to: Steck-Vaughn Company, P.O. Box 26015, Austin, TX 78755.

Library of Congress Cataloging-in-Publication Data

Nugent, Nicholas.
    Pakistan and Bangladesh / Nicholas Nugent.
      p.   cm.—(World in view)
    Includes index.
    Summary: Introduces the history, people, and way of life of Pakistan and Bangladesh.
    ISBN 0-8114-2456-1
    1. Pakistan—Juvenile literature. 2. Bangladesh—Juvenile literature. [1. Pakistan. 2. Bangladesh.] I. Title. II. Series.
DS376.9.N84   1993   92-10765
945.9—dc20   CIP AC

Cover: *The Shalainan Gardens, laid out in 1637 by the Mogul emperor Shah Jahan, are found six miles east of Lahore.*
Title page: *Nomads and camel train, Baluchistan.*

Design by Julian Holland Publishing Ltd.

Typeset by Multifacit Graphics, Keyport, NJ
Printed and bound in the United States
by Lake Book, Melrose Park, IL
1 2 3 4 5 6 7 8 9 0 LB 98 97 96 95 94 93

Photographic credits:
The photographs on pages 9, 13, 15, 34, 40, 41, 49, 53, 58, 63, 64, 68, 69, 70, 80, 81, 88, 90, and 92 are by courtesy of the Ministry of Information, Bangladesh Government.
The remaining photographs are: Cover: ©Ric Ergenbright; title page: J. Allan Cash; 7 Serajur Rahman; 10 J. Allan Cash; 11 Robert Harding Picture Library; 17 Nicholas Nugent; 21 Mary Evans Picture Library; 22 Hulton-Deutsch Collection; 27 Nicholas Nugent; 29 Paul Popper Ltd; 31, 32 Hulton-Deutsch Collection; 37 Nicholas Nugent; 38 Nigel Blythe/Robert Harding Picture Library; 44 Nicholas Nugent; 45 Nigel Blythe/Robert Harding Picture Library; 52 Robert Harding Picture Library; 55 Nicholas Nugent; 57 Serajur Rahman; 60, 66 Robert Harding Picture Library; 73 J. Allan Cash; 74 Nicholas Nugent; 76, 78 J. Allan Cash; 84 Nicholas Nugent; 86 Sporting Pics (UK) Ltd; 87 J. Allan Cash.

Contents

1. Introducing Pakistan and Bangladesh   5
2. Four Thousand Years of History   14
3. Independence and After   26
4. Religion   36
5. People of Pakistan and Bangladesh   41
6. The Way of Life   49
7. Farming and Fishing   58
8. Industry, Trade, and Energy   65
9. Transportation and Communications   72
10. Health, Education, and Welfare   79
11. Sports, Leisure, and the Arts   85
12. Pakistan and Bangladesh Today   90
    Index   95

PAKISTAN AND BANGLADESH

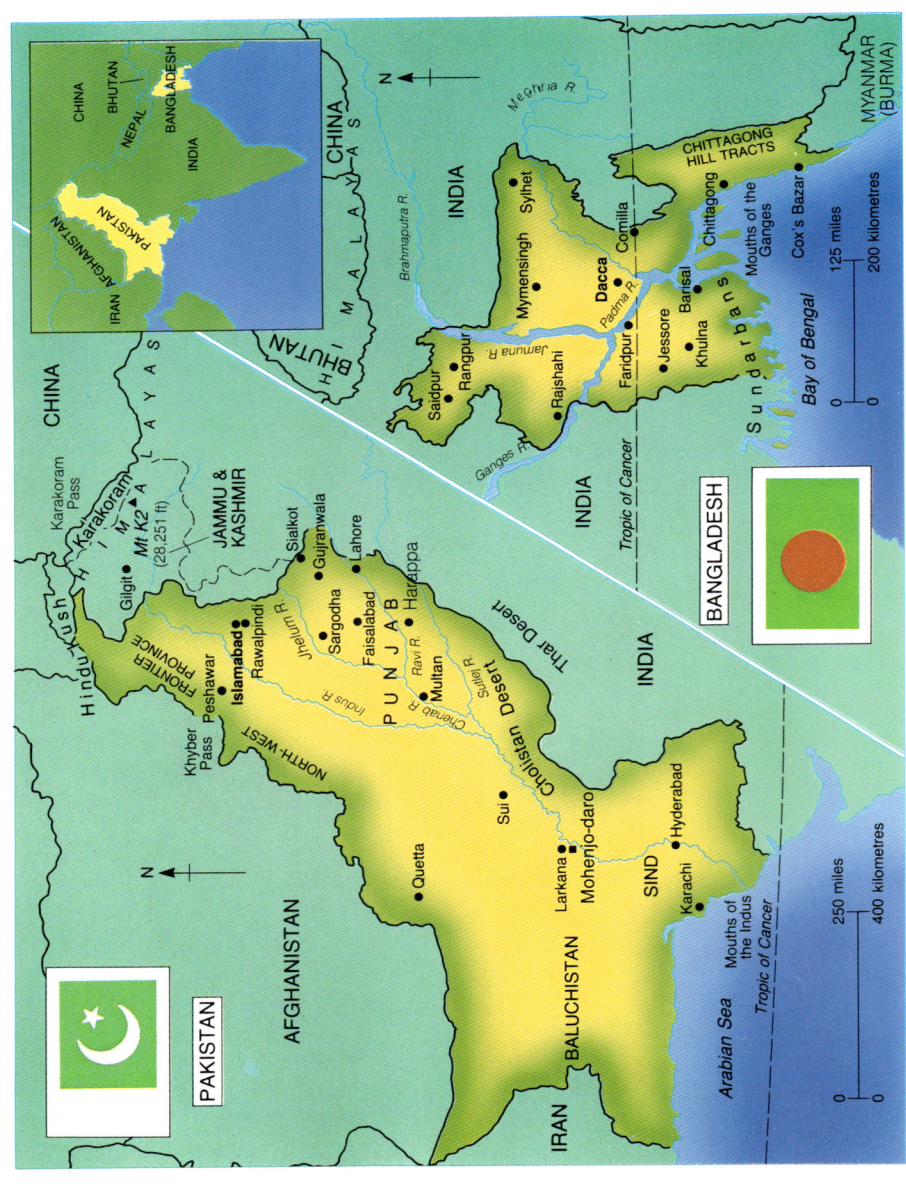

1 Introducing Pakistan and Bangladesh

Pakistan and Bangladesh are two Asian nations situated on opposite sides of India. With India they form a huge landmass known as the Indian subcontinent. Pakistan, the larger of the two, lies northwest of India. Excluding territory that is disputed with India, it has a land area of 307,292 square miles (796,095 square kilometers). This is about twice the size of California or about 85 percent of British Columbia. To the west Pakistan has a short border with Iran and a much longer border with Afghanistan. There is a long border with India to the east, and a short border with

Fact Box

	Pakistan	Bangladesh
Area:	307,292 sq mi (796,095 sq km)	55,598 sq mi (143,998 sq km)
Population:	113 million (estimated)	118 million (estimated)
Capital city:	Islamabad	Dacca
Member of:	United Nations, The Commonwealth, South Asian Association for Regional Cooperation	United Nations, The Commonwealth, South Asian Association for Regional Cooperation
Currency:	rupee = 100 paisa	taka = 100 paisa
National language:	Urdu	Bengali
Religion:	Islam	Islam
Official name:	The Islamic Republic of Pakistan (1947)	People's Republic of Bangladesh (1971)

PAKISTAN AND BANGLADESH

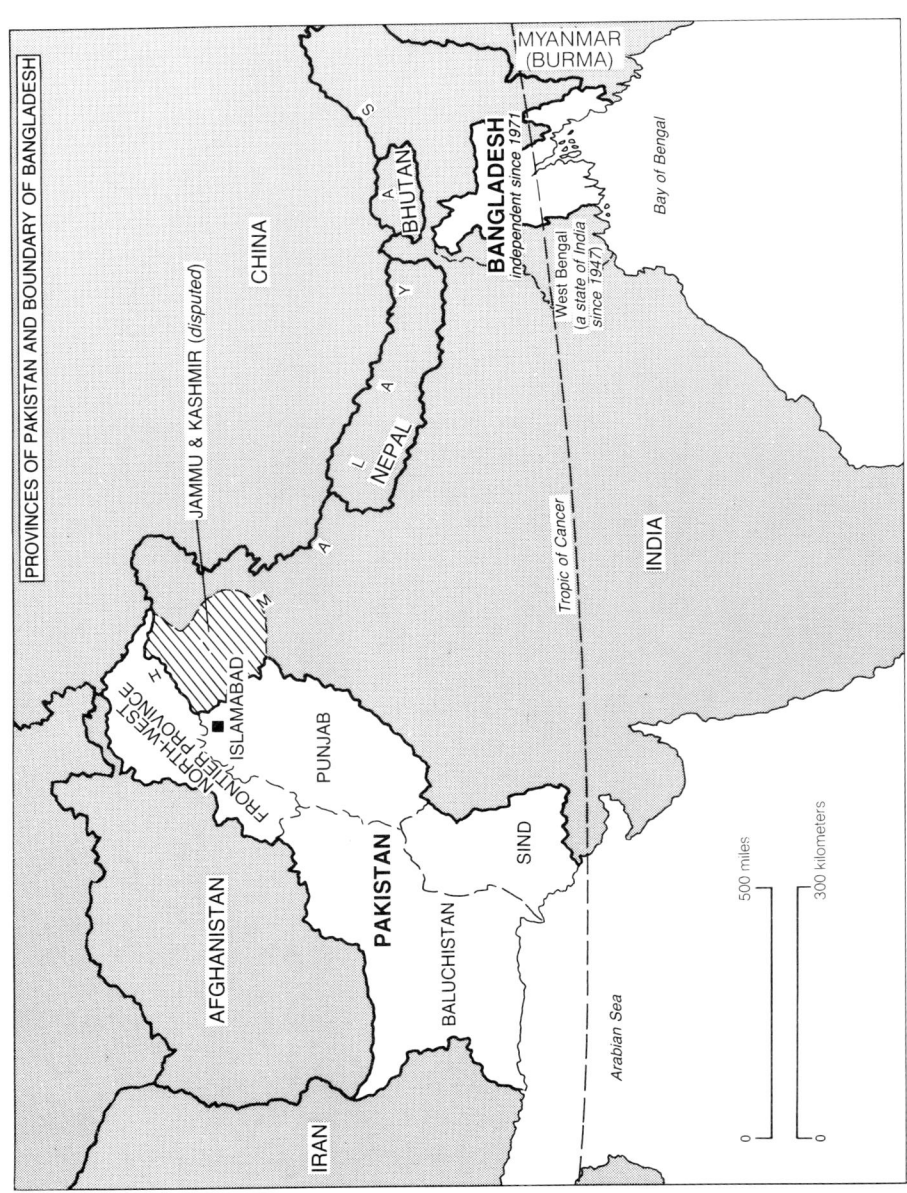

INTRODUCING PAKISTAN AND BANGLADESH

China in the northern region of Kashmir. Both India and Pakistan claim Kashmir as their own.

Bangladesh lies northeast of India. Apart from its coastline and a short border with Myanmar (Burma) in the southeast of the country, Bangladesh is encircled by its huge neighbor, India. Its 55,598 square miles (143,998 square kilometers) is equivalent in size to the state of Illinois or twice the size of New Brunswick, Canada. In land area Bangladesh is less than 20 percent the size of Pakistan, yet the population of both countries is about the same. Around 110 million people live in Bangladesh and 120 million in Pakistan. This large population in a relatively small area makes Bangladesh one of the most densely populated countries in the world. The situation is made worse because much of

Bangladesh is a very low-lying country. Much of the dry land in this picture will disappear in the rainy season, when the river level rises rapidly and floods the surrounding area.

Bangladesh lies below sea level, so it is subject to flooding. In the rainy season a large part of the country simply disappears under water.

The great rivers
Pakistan and Bangladesh lie at opposite ends of the lowland region that stretches across northern India. Several of the world's longest rivers flow across this great plain, including the Indus and the Ganges from which the region takes its name, the Indo-Gangetic Plain. The Indus and its tributaries, the Jhelum, Chenab, Ravi, and Sutlej, are the main sources of water for the people, livestock, and crops of Pakistan. The Indus takes its name from Sind, the area of southern Pakistan where it flows into the Arabian Sea. Most of the people of Pakistan live in the fertile areas surrounding these rivers. The rivers have provided a name for Pakistan's most densely populated province, the Punjab, which means "the land of five rivers."

Bangladesh is even more dominated by rivers. They provide the country with fertile agricultural land but also use up precious land on which people might otherwise live. The Ganges River joins the Brahmaputra and Jamuna rivers to form the Padma. This in turn joins with the Meghna. Together they flow into the sea through one enormous delta, known as the Mouths of the Ganges. The swampy forested area where they arrive at the Bay of Bengal is known as the Sundarbans.

The rivers of Pakistan and Bangladesh rise high in the Himalayas, the towering mountain range that overlooks the Indo-Gangetic Plain like an

INTRODUCING PAKISTAN AND BANGLADESH

The numerous rivers of Bangladesh join to make a huge swampy region called the Mouths of the Ganges. People can live on the thousands of small islands in these regions, but space for housing is very limited.

enormous giant. The rivers carry the waters of the melting Himalayan snows hundreds of miles through the plains to the Arabian Sea in the west and the Bay of Bengal in the east.

High and low

The north of Pakistan is dominated by the Himalayan Mountains. Some of the world's highest mountains are in the part of the state of Kashmir that is controlled by Pakistan. K2, also called Mount Godwin Austen, is the second tallest mountain in the world, standing at a height of 28,251 feet (8,611 meters). Only Mount Everest, in Nepal, is higher. The section of the Himalayas along Pakistan's border with China is called the Karakoram Range, while the

PAKISTAN AND BANGLADESH

The fertile Hunza valley is in the Himalayan Mountains, which dominate northern Pakistan. In the background is Mount Rakaposhi, whose snow-covered slopes form part of the Karakoram Range. The mountain is 25,000 feet (7,620 meters) high.

mountains stretching into Afghanistan are called the Hindu Kush. Bangladesh has few mountains of its own, except the Chittagong Hill Tracts in the extreme southeastern part of the country. The highest peak, Mount Keokradong, is only 4,035 feet (1,230 meters) high. Otherwise, it is a low-lying land that is all too frequently swamped when the river waters rise and break their banks.

The landscape in southern Pakistan is in complete contrast to that in the north. The Indus River flows between two deserts. On its eastern bank lies the great Thar Desert, which stretches far inside India. The part in Pakistan is called the Cholistan Desert. To the west the rugged plateau of Baluchistan stretches as a sparsely populated wilderness south of Afghanistan to border

INTRODUCING PAKISTAN AND BANGLADESH

Iranian Baluchistan. This important border with Iran has meant that much of the Iranian, or Persian, culture and language has been absorbed into Pakistan's own culture.

Problems with rainfall

The Tropic of Cancer, the northern limit of the tropical region, runs just to the south of Pakistan. It passes through the center of Bangladesh near its capital, Dacca. Both Pakistan and Bangladesh are hot countries, although winter snow falls regularly in the northern part of Pakistan and remains on the mountaintops all year round. Rainfall is not evenly spread, and much of southern Pakistan (the provinces of Sind and

Baluchistan in southern Pakistan is a desert region. The steep gullies have almost no vegetation, and the riverbeds are largely dry. Very few people live in this region.

Baluchistan) remains dry all year and is unsuitable for growing crops.

If Pakistan has too little rain, Bangladesh tends to have too much rain, or too much falling within a short period. Sometimes the monsoon, or seasonal rainfall, is accompanied by severe tropical winds called cyclones. The sudden increase in the amount of water often causes the rivers to flood the land. However, Bangladeshis are grateful for the monsoon, which occurs between June and October, since it enables large quantities of rice and other crops to be grown.

Wildlife
Bangladesh's climate enables it to support a wide variety of vegetation, including the fabulous Sundarbans mangrove swamps, where all kinds of trees grow. The Sundarbans are also home to a variety of wildlife. Leopards are found in Bangladesh, as well as jackals, mongooses, and several varieties of monkeys and bears. Elephants are found in the Chittagong Hill Tracts, where they are used as beasts of burden.

Pakistan, with its much greater variety of climate and vegetation, has monkeys and bears, as well as jackals, hyenas, foxes, and the rare snow leopard but no tigers or elephants. Instead, camels can be seen transporting goods and passengers across the desert wastelands or even plowing the fields in the south. Crocodiles and snakes are found in both countries, and the seas off both coasts are rich in aquatic life.

INTRODUCING PAKISTAN AND BANGLADESH

The Bengal Tiger
The Bengal tiger inhabits the swampy forest on the delta land of southern Bangladesh known as the Sundarbans. It is one of the most brightly colored species of tiger, with reddish tan and black stripes across its back and a whitish belly. Tigers grow to a length of more than 10 feet (3 meters), including a 3-foot (1-meter) tail, to a height of about 3 feet at the shoulder, and to more than 500 pounds (250 kilograms). The tiger is an endangered species, and the number still living in Bangladesh is unknown. The color of its coat makes it hard to spot in the thick jungle.

2 Four Thousand Years of History

Archaeologists have found evidence that Stone Age humans lived 6,000 years ago in the lands now known as Pakistan and Bangladesh. The first inhabitants of the region about whom we have much information lived in the Indus Valley region of southern Pakistan about 4,000 years ago. At Mohenjo-Daro, not far from the Pakistani city of Hyderabad, lie the remains of a large city. The name Mohenjo-Daro means "the mound of the dead." From what is left of the streets, buildings, and drainage channels we can tell that the people of the Indus Valley civilization had a highly developed way of life. The well-planned city shows evidence of public baths and community centers. Houses were built around a central courtyard. Stone and iron tools found at the site prove that the Indus Valley people knew how to farm, fish, and hunt. Remains of coins, toys, and animal-drawn carts have also been found.

Another ancient site dating from around the same time has been discovered farther up the Indus Valley, at Harappa near the Indian frontier. The people who lived in the Indus Valley around 2500 B.C. might have traded with inhabitants of two other early civilizations that were located in Egypt and Mesopotamia (present-day Iraq).

The Aryans and Hinduism
There are different theories as to why the Indus Valley people abandoned their cities. Some

FOUR THOUSAND YEARS OF HISTORY

experts say the cities were destroyed when invaders attacked. Others believe that a change in the climate caused the settlers to move elsewhere. Today Mohenjo-Daro is in one of the driest areas of Pakistan, and few crops grow there. The Indus River has changed its course and flows some distance from the ancient site.

Some centuries after the decline of the Indus Valley civilization, a new group of invaders arrived at the western end of the Indo-Gangetic Plain. They were the Aryans, who arrived overland from the west. They probably originated from what is now Iran. At first the Aryans settled in the Punjab, which was renowned even then for its fertile soil. Later they spread their settlements throughout the Indo-

These are the ruins of the Somapuri Vihara, a very large Buddhist monastery built at Paharpur in the eighth century A.D. There was room for nearly 200 monks in the monastery.

Gangetic Plain, as far east as what is now Bangladesh. The Aryans were to give India its main religion of Hinduism, which emerged out of their epic poem, the *Rig-Veda*, and two epic legends, the *Mahabharata* and *Ramayana*. These still remain the most important books for Hindus.

Although the Aryans were to establish Hinduism as the main religion of the Indian subcontinent, it did not take hold until after the coming of a great ruler, Asoka. Asoka had followed the teachings of Buddha, who founded the Buddhist religion. Asoka is remembered as the first person to unite most of the subcontinent under one ruler.

The Arabs and Islam
The Indus Valley people and the Aryans were followed by the Arabs, who arrived in the southern part of the Indus Valley in the eighth century. They had journeyed overland from the Arab capital of Damascus, now in Syria. These settlers are especially important in the history of Pakistan because they brought the religion of Islam. The Arabs were followers of a prophet called Muhammad, who had lived on the Arabian Peninsula at the beginning of the seventh century. They called themselves Muhammadans, or Muslims. The Islamic religion is based on the *Koran*, the holy book that contains the words of the Muslim God, Allah, as related by the Prophet Muhammad.

Before the arrival of the Arabs, parts of the Indus Valley had been incorporated into the Persian Empire, where the religion of Islam was

FOUR THOUSAND YEARS OF HISTORY

already practiced. It was the invaders from Syria who made the greater impact on the areas of Sind, which they conquered, because they converted the local people to their religion. This was the time at which the Muslim religion was spreading in several directions. Muslim Arabs from North Africa had succeeded in conquering Spain, although other followers of Islam were repelled when they tried to conquer Greece from Turkey. In their eastward journey, the Arabs were content to take control of the rich farmland of Sind.

The growth of Islam

Islam spread farther eastward 300 years later when the Muslim rulers of the Afghan kingdom of Ghazni captured Lahore, the capital of the Punjab, and then Delhi. Delhi was an important

The spread of Islam resulted in the building of numerous mosques, such as the Badshahi Mosque in Lahore. On this misty morning the large courtyard rings with the hammering of stonemasons as they repair the mosque, which was built by the Mogul Emperor Alamgir, also known as Aurangzeb, around 1674.

settlement on the Indo-Gangetic Plain. After the Afghans set themselves up as kings of Delhi, they tried to expand their influence and control eastward into places that were at the time part of the Mauyra Empire. Around the year 1200 they succeeded in conquering Bengal, where they found a people who were willing to convert in order to become followers of Muhammad. In this way, Islam was introduced into Bengal, part of which now forms Bangladesh and part of which is now the state of West Bengal in India.

The history of the Indian subcontinent is a complex story in which successive waves of invaders arrived to dominate the existing settlers, until in time the power of each group declined. In due course, the power of the kings of Delhi declined, and some of the lesser Hindu rulers became more powerful once again. It took another invasion to bring the Muslim religion once more to the fore. For the second time almost the entire subcontinent was united under one dynasty, or ruling family. This time it was the Moguls who formed a Muslim dynasty.

Mogul rule
Mogul rule of the Indian subcontinent started with an invasion from the north, from Central Asia, by Timur "the lame," or Tamberlane. He swept down with 90,000 men and horses to overthrow the king of Delhi. He had already conquered Persia and Afghanistan and wanted to extend his empire eastward.

Tamberlane's descendant, Babur, was the first Mogul ruler. At first his empire stretched from Baluchistan and Sind in the west to Bengal in the east. Babur's grandson, Akbar, strengthened Mogul rule during the latter part of the sixteenth century, conquering Hindu kingdoms in the south. Akbar's grandson was Shah Jahan, who built the Taj Mahal at Agra in India, one of the most famous monuments in the world. A fine example of Mogul architecture in Pakistan is the Badshahi Mosque in Lahore. Evidence of Mogul influence in architecture can also be found in Bangladesh.

The arrival of the British
All the time Mogul rulers were on the throne in Delhi they were resisting invasions by other challengers, including the Afghans, who several times tried to regain the throne. At the same time the Mogul rulers were strengthening and extending their control. They dominated the subcontinent until long after the British set up trading posts early in the seventeenth century.

The British were only interested in trading at first. They wanted spices and other agricultural products that were not available in Europe. One of the areas with which they were most interested in trading was Bengal, where the Moguls granted them some land.

The British had European rivals, such as the French, against whom they fought several battles. At the Battle of Plassey in 1757 the British defeated a local ruler, the Nawab of Bengal, and established control over the rich province of Bengal. Warren Hastings became the first British governor-general of Bengal. Hastings refused to pay taxes to the Moguls. He had effectively ended the Mogul rule of Bengal.

The downfall of the Moguls

Mogul rule was in decline elsewhere, too. The British, who had at first been content to set up trading posts and to trade with local rulers, began to fight to extend their control. They took over more territory for themselves, often displacing local rulers in the process.

A famous conquest was that of Sind. Accusing the local rulers, the *amirs*, of disloyalty to the British, General Charles Napier set out to take control of Sind in 1843. After defeating the amirs at the Battle of Miani, he sent a message to Britain containing the Latin word *peccavi*, which means "I have sinned." The British rulers understood the pun. He meant "I have captured Sind." Napier was rewarded with a knighthood and made governor of Sind. Six years later another area brought under British rule was the Punjab, which had been ruled by Sikhs, warriorlike followers of a religion that they had established in the province.

From 1857 to 1859, shortly after Sind and the Punjab came under British rule, there was an uprising against the British in north India by *sepoys*, Indian soldiers serving in the British Indian army. Indians call it their First War of Independence; the British refer to it as the Sepoy Rebellion. It provided the excuse the British needed to end Mogul rule in the subcontinent once and for all. The British sent the last Mogul ruler, Bahadur Shah II, into exile at Rangoon in Burma and established their first viceroy, Charles John Canning, who ruled India on behalf of Queen Victoria. She was proclaimed Empress of India. Mogul India had finally given way to

FOUR THOUSAND YEARS OF HISTORY

Calcutta was the seat of British rule in India. It was the capital of the state of Bengal. The British influence affected many aspects of life, including architecture, as shown in this photograph of Clive Street in the 1890s.

British India. In 1911 the seat of British rule was transferred from Calcutta, the capital of the province of Bengal, to Delhi, which had been the seat of the Mogul rulers.

Freedom movements

The uprising of 1857 was an expression of the discontent Indians felt at having a distant European nation take control of their country. This latest wave of invaders had made a mark on the entire subcontinent. The end of the nineteenth century saw the formation of political movements demanding an end to British rule. The main one was the Indian National Congress. The Muslim League, founded to protect the interests of Muslim Indians, was also

PAKISTAN AND BANGLADESH

Jawaharlal Nehru and Muhammad Ali Jinnah (wearing the European suit) were leaders in the struggle for India's freedom from British rule, but Jinnah insisted on the creation of the new state of Pakistan. This photograph was taken in 1946 after a meeting held to discuss the problems.

campaigning for freedom. Freedom fighters like Mohandas K. Gandhi, Jawaharlal Nehru, and Muhammad Ali Jinnah emerged to lead what was, for the most part, a peaceful struggle for what they called "home rule." Mohandas Gandhi, for example, led a peaceful "salt march" to the sea in his home state of Gujarat to protest the British order that said tax had to be paid on

> **Muhammad Ali Jinnah**
> Muhammad Ali Jinnah, who is known as Quaid-I-Azam or Great Leader, is regarded as the father of Pakistan. A London-educated lawyer, he supported calls by the Indian National Congress for an end to British rule of India. However, he feared that independent India would be dominated by the Hindu majority under leaders like Mohandas Gandhi and Jawaharlal Nehru, so he led calls for a separate Muslim homeland to be carved out of India. When the British eventually agreed to leave the Indian subcontinent in August 1947, they handed over power to the separate independent states of India and Pakistan. Muhammad Ali Jinnah became the first governor-general of the new republic of Pakistan but tragically died a year after independence. The Muslim League remains one of the major parties in Pakistan.

salt from the shoreline. Gandhi and 100,000 others were arrested for defying British laws.

Partition

In the 1930s a split in the freedom movement took place. Muslims led by Muhammad Ali Jinnah began to be concerned that British rule would be replaced by Indian rule in which Hindus would occupy the most powerful positions. If that was what was going to come with independence, they wanted to have a nation of their own. At Lahore in 1940, members of the Muslim League passed a resolution calling for the creation of their own Muslim nation, to be called Pakistan. Leaders of congress argued that India should remain united

PAKISTAN AND BANGLADESH

> **How Pakistan Got Its Name**
> The name "Pakistan" was thought up by Muslim students studying at Cambridge, England, in the 1930s. It is derived from the names of the Muslim areas that they wanted to separate from India to form a new nation: **P**unjab; **A**fghania, the area bordering Afghanistan; **K**ashmir, the princely state that Pakistan continues to dispute with India; **S**ind; and Baluchis**TAN**—or PAKiSTAN. In Urdu, *pak* means "pure," and *stan* means "land"—so there were two reasons for calling their new Muslim nation Pakistan.

after independence, but Muslim leaders were determined to have a nation of their own. When the British finally left India in 1947, the subcontinent was divided into two independent states, Pakistan and India. Pakistan was split into two parts, with over 1,000 miles (about 1,800 kilometers) of India between them. In the eastern half was part of the province of Bengal and in the west the states of Baluchistan, Sind, North-West Frontier Province, and half of the state of the Punjab, which was divided between India and Pakistan. In all these areas, Muslims were in the majority.

Kashmir

Many Muslims left their homes in north India to migrate to Pakistan, just as Hindus and Sikhs migrated in the other direction toward India. Many other Muslims stayed put, and today there are as many Muslims in India as there are in either Bangladesh or Pakistan. What is called the "partition" of the subcontinent caused a confrontation in relations between followers of the three religions. Many people were massacred as they made the journey to their new homelands.

The state of Kashmir, where Muslims were in a majority but whose ruler was a Hindu, was disputed between India and Pakistan. The two countries went to war, resulting in the state being split between them. More than 40 years later, the state is still split, and the dispute between India and Pakistan, each claiming ownership of Kashmir, has not been resolved.

3 Independence and After

From the beginning, Pakistan was an unwieldy nation. The separation of Bengali East Pakistan from West Pakistan by such a huge distance was aggravated by the bad relations that existed between India and Pakistan. This bad feeling arose out of the bloody separation of the two countries. Indians blamed Pakistanis for forcing the partition of the subcontinent. Pakistanis said they resented the way the Indians had chased Muslims out and seized their property. Both countries also blamed the British for allowing bloody massacres to take place and for failing to settle some of the details of the separation, such as which country should have Kashmir.

A troubled beginning
Pakistan, as a new nation, lacked many of the resources of India, even though the army was shared by both countries. It lacked a capital city, as Delhi was in India. It also lacked a parliament building and other national institutions. It was a country without a center. Possibly for this reason Pakistan had more difficulty establishing its new independent government. Another reason was that the nation's founder, Muhammad Ali Jinnah, who had become Pakistan's first governor-general, died just a year after independence. His death was a bad enough blow for the new nation struggling to establish itself, but three years later it first prime minister, Liaquat Ali Khan, was

INDEPENDENCE AND AFTER

For many years Pakistan lacked a parliament building. Each province had its own provincial assembly, such as this one in Lahore.

assassinated. A whole succession of prime ministers followed, none of whom lasted long. There was also some confusion between the roles of the governor-general, the country's head of state, and the prime minister, who could be dismissed by the governor-general. The biggest problem for the new nation was deciding how it should be governed.

Several prime ministers of Pakistan came from the eastern wing of the country. And although East Pakistan had the larger population (about 54 percent, compared to 46 percent in the western wing), the politicians from West Pakistan held most of the power. In 1956 a change to the Constitution, which states the basic laws of the country, ensured that the two wings of the country were equally represented in the National Assembly, or parliament. West Pakistanis did not want to be dominated by the numerically greater Bengalis. Other changes made Pakistan an Islamic republic in name only and replaced the governor-general with a president, who was to exercise only reserve, or mostly symbolic, powers. Real control of the country was in the hands of the prime minister.

The new Constitution did not last long. After continued quarreling between political parties, the president suspended the Constitution in 1958, abolished political parties, and imposed martial law. This move meant that the army took over the running of the country. The army leader, General Ayub Khan, became president. This was the first of several periods during which Pakistan has been ruled by the army rather than by politicians. Field Marshal Ayub Khan (as he later became known) ruled the country for more than ten years before handing over power to another soldier, General Yahya Khan.

East and West Pakistan
It was under General Yahya Khan that the split between the two wings of Pakistan took place. Resentment in East Pakistan had gradually increased as West Pakistan seemed to receive more in development funds and foreign aid. Inhabitants of the eastern wing felt that the money Pakistan earned by selling its tea and jute to other countries was being used to pay for the development of the western wing. Resentment came to a head when the western wing secured money from abroad to build hydroelectric plants

INDEPENDENCE AND AFTER

Guerrillas supporting the Awami League celebrate as the government of West Pakistan surrenders in December 1971. They are displaying a photograph of Sheikh Mujibur Rahman, who became prime minister of the newly created Bangladesh.

in the Indus Valley that offered no benefits to the eastern wing. There was also resentment at attempts by West Pakistanis to impose Urdu as the official language even on the Bengalis of the east wing.

The crisis in relations between the two wings of the divided country grew after the main political party in the eastern wing, the Awami League, won more than half the seats in the National Assembly in the elections held in December 1970. This meant that by rights, the Awami League leader, Sheikh Mujibur Rahman, or Sheikh Mujib as he was commonly called, should have become Pakistan's prime minister. The problem was that Sheikh Mujib had fought and won the elections by demanding that the eastern wing take charge of their own affairs. He and the Awami League

29

> **Sheikh Mujibur Rahman**
> Sheikh Mujibur Rahman (or Sheikh Mujib) is considered to be the father of the Bangladeshi nation. His political opponents believe he lost his right to this title because of the harsh way he ruled the country after it broke away from Pakistan under his leadership. Like so many other political leaders in Pakistan, Sheikh Mujib was trained as a lawyer and took part in the struggle against British rule in the 1940s. In March 1971 Sheikh Mujib declared Bangladesh independent, four months after the Awami League had won an overwhelming victory in Pakistan's general election. The Awami League had called for autonomy, or self-rule, for the eastern wing of the country. Sheikh Mujib was imprisoned in West Pakistan, but after Indian and Bangladeshi forces defeated the Pakistani army he was released. He flew back to a hero's welcome in Bangladesh and became Bangladesh's first prime minister and then president. His rule was short-lived. In August 1975 soldiers stormed into his house in Dacca and shot and killed him, his wife, and many other members of his family. His daughter, Sheikh Hasina, who was abroad at the time, escaped. She became leader of the Awami League and has been campaigning for the party to come to power again.

wanted the Bengali people to be responsible for all important decisions affecting their wing of the country. They felt there should be only a loose link with West Pakistan and that the two wings should have separate parliaments. This was not acceptable to the leaders of the western wing.

INDEPENDENCE AND AFTER

Independent Bangladesh

After the eastern wing declared its independence from Pakistan in March 1971, civil war loomed. Many Pakistanis from the western wing were serving in the eastern wing, and many Bengalis were in West Pakistan. Fighting broke out between the army, led by General Yahya Khan, and the people of East Pakistan. When the fighting began in December 1971, millions of Bengalis took refuge across the border in India as the Pakistani army went to war against the guerrilla forces trying to achieve East Pakistan's independence. The Indian army joined the war on the side of the new nation, making Pakistan's

During the civil war in 1971, millions of refugees left East Pakistan. They virtually swamped the border towns in the surrounding Indian states.

31

PAKISTAN AND BANGLADESH

defeat inevitable. The war was short but bloody. The result was that Pakistan was cut in half, and the new nation of Bangladesh took its place on the subcontinent. The subcontinent had been partitioned for the second time.

How Bangladesh Got Its Name

Bangla is the local name for the Bengali people and *desh* means "land," so Bangladesh means simply "the land of the Bengalis." This name was chosen by the nation's founders when they broke away from Pakistan in 1971. Almost all the people of Bangladesh are Bengalis, but not all Bengalis live in Bangladesh. In 1947 the province of Bengal had been split into two states—the eastern half formed East Pakistan, which later became Bangladesh. Many Muslims migrated to the eastern wing to live in the new Muslim nation. The western half formed the Indian state of West Bengal. It is home to both Hindu and Muslim Bengalis.

Sheikh Mujibur Rahman at a press conference in 1972, soon after the new nation of Bangladesh was created.

INDEPENDENCE AND AFTER

The new Pakistan
The new, smaller Pakistan may have been easier to rule, but it still had its difficulties. General Yahya Khan accepted responsibility for the military defeat and handed over power to an elected politician, Zulfikar Ali Bhutto, who became the most influential leader Pakistan has had. Zulfikar Ali Bhutto promised to improve living conditions for the poor people. However, in 1977 he was thrown out of office by another army takeover led by General Zia-ul-Haq. Zulfikar Ali Bhutto was accused of ordering the murder of a political opponent and was later executed. His execution aroused protests in Pakistan and around the world.

Benazir Bhutto
General Zia, a devout Muslim, changed the law to make Pakistan more of an Islamic state and strengthened its ties with the Muslim countries of the Middle East. He was in no hurry to restore elections and representative or democratic government to Pakistan. When he finally did hold elections, he refused to allow political parties to function and stayed on as president. In 1988 General Zia was killed in a plane crash in the east of Pakistan.

In the elections that followed his death, political parties were allowed to function. Zulfikar Ali Bhutto's daughter, Benazir Bhutto, led the Pakistan People's Party to victory and became prime minister. But, two years later the new president, Ghulam Ishaq Khan, dismissed Benazir Bhutto and called for new elections in which the other main party came to power under

PAKISTAN AND BANGLADESH

Prime Minister Nawaz Sharif. The dismissal of Benazir Bhutto showed that the president of Pakistan is the most powerful person in the land. The army has also continued to play an important role in running the country.

Bangladesh

After Bangladesh's painful birth as a nation, Sheikh Mujibur Rahman was the undisputed leader of the new country. He believed Bangladesh should be a country in which all religions were regarded equally, not one in which Islam had a special place. Still, Sheikh Mujib's rule became increasingly authoritarian, and he abolished all political parties except for his own Awami League. Four years after Bangladesh's independence, Sheikh Mujib was shot dead. An

The impressive Jatiya Sangsad, or National Assembly of Bangladesh, dominates the skyline of the capital city of Dacca.

army chief, General Ziaur Rahman, took over until he in turn was murdered by fellow army officers. The next army general to rule was General H. Ershad, who ruled for the longest period. Like General Zia in Pakistan, General Ershad held elections and then refused demands that he step down and allow elected politicans to take over. He also made it clear that he would continue to use the army because he believed it had an important role to fulfill in running the country. Eventually, General Ershad was forced out of office in 1990 when it became clear that he had lost the support of the army. In March 1991 Khaleda Zia, the widow of General Ziaur Rahman and the leader of the Bangladesh Nationalist Party, won the country's first free and fair elections. She became Bangladesh's first woman prime minister.

The Commonwealth
After Bangladesh declared independence from Pakistan, the new nation was welcomed into the Commonwealth, an organization that links nations that were once ruled by Britain. Pakistan's rulers were so upset by this decision that they withdrew from the Commonwealth in protest. After General Zia's death, Benazir Bhutto negotiated Pakistan's reentry into the Commonwealth. Today not only have Pakistan and Bangladesh become friends again, forgetting the tensions of the past, but both are fellow members of the Commonwealth.

4 Religion

Pakistan separated from India over the issue of religion, so it is not surprising that the vast majority of its people are Muslims. The 3 percent of Pakistanis who are not Muslims belong to either the country's very small community of Hindus, to Karachi's Parsi community, or have converted to Christianity. Most Hindus fled to India when the subcontinent was partitioned, just as many Muslims who were living in what is now India migrated to Pakistan.

Worship and tradition
Muslims follow the holy book known as the Koran, which represents the word of their God, Allah, as related by the Prophet Muhammad. Muslims worship in mosques. Even small villages in Pakistan have mosques, with their distinctive onion-shaped domes. A *muezzin*, or mosque official, calls the faithful to prayer several times a day, usually over a loudspeaker. The priest who leads the prayers at the mosque is called an *imam*. Faithful Muslims are expected to pray five times each day, facing in the direction of the holy city of Mecca in Saudi Arabia. Mecca was the birthplace of the Prophet Muhammad, who founded Islam. Devout Muslims are expected to try to make the pilgrimage to Mecca, known as the *hajj*, at least once in their lifetime.

It is the custom in Islamic countries for women to remain in *purdah*, or out of sight of men who are not their husbands. This means they wear a veil in public places or stay in the inner rooms when

RELIGION

Mosques are found throughout Pakistan and Bangladesh. This one in northern Pakistan has a post office in the basement.

visitors come to the house. City dwellers in Pakistan are not particularly strict about the rules of purdah, but in some parts of the countryside it is rare to see women not covered by a black gown, known as a *burqa*, and veil. Islamic tradition dictates that the primary role of women is to stay at home and be dutiful wives and mothers. This has not prevented some women from rising to the

37

top in their chosen fields. Benazir Bhutto became the first woman prime minister of a muslim country.

Islam in conflict

In recent years Pakistan has become more Islamic. Some of its laws have changed to conform to Islamic practice. This is reflected in its official name, the Islamic Republic of Pakistan. Some priests and scholars would like to see this trend continue. They believe that Islam is an important force for holding together the different

Most Muslims in Pakistan and Bangladesh are Sunni Muslims, but there are a small number of Shiite Muslims, such as these outside a mosque in Karachi.

peoples that make up Pakistan. They want the laws of Islam to be given a dominant position so that the National Assembly is not allowed to introduce laws that conflict with Islam. Such moves are backed by some of the political parties, including the Muslim League. Opponents say that Muhammad Ali Jinnah, who founded both the Muslim League and Pakistan, had not planned to create a Muslim state, only one where Muslims were in a majority and were not subordinated to Hindus.

The same debate between those wanting an Islamic state and those who favor a state ruled by elected government rather than religion has raged in Bangladesh. As in Pakistan, most people in Bangladesh are followers of Islam; Bangladesh is about 85 percent Muslim. Most of the rest are Hindus who did not migrate to India when eastern Bengal was separated from India in 1947. There are also some Christians, and some of the tribal communities living in the Chittagong Hill Tracts are Buddhists.

Religion and independence
In a sense the rebellion of the people of the former East Pakistan against West Pakistan in 1971 proved that religion alone cannot unite two different peoples who are geographically separated. Although the people of Bangladesh are faithful Muslims, in 1971 they felt their Bengali language and race were more important. This was how they justified becoming a nation in their own right.

Bangladeshis today observe their religion as they always have, through prayer, pilgrimage,

PAKISTAN AND BANGLADESH

Hindus in Bangladesh celebrating Ratha Jatra, one of their important religious rites. There are about 13 million Hindus in Bangladesh.

and the observance of other practices and traditions, which, for example, forbid them to eat the meat of the pig, considered to be an unclean animal. As in Pakistan, Friday, the Muslim holy day, is observed as the day of rest and prayer. It is the day when many people visit the mosque. Although proud of their Islamic heritage, Bangladeshis also pride themselves on the fact that non-Muslims play a full part in the life of the country and can and do rise to some of the highest positions in Bangladesh.

5 People of Pakistan and Bangladesh

The vast majority of the people of Bangladesh, around 98 percent, are Bengalis. They speak the Bengali language and are closely related to the Bengalis of India. An Indian Bengali would have no difficulty talking to a Bangladeshi Bengali. They would read the same books and would certainly watch the same movies. Bengalis from Bangladesh have migrated into northeastern India in search of work or land to farm. Many have settled in the Indian states of Assam and Tripura. For similar economic reasons, other Bangladeshis have settled in the Middle East, the United States, and Britain, where they have established large communities in London, New

These Bengali girls are learning textile printing. Bengalis are said to be descendants of Dravidians, the earliest inhabitants of India. They were driven to the east of the subcontinent by the Aryans.

York, Abu Dhabi, Dubai, and Saudi Arabia. Most of the Bangladeshis in North America first came as a result of political problems, but recently more have been seeking better economic conditions. Almost all are professionals or white-collar workers and have settled in U.S. and Canadian urban centers.

The tribal groups

Around the border of the country, and especially in the Chittagong Hills of southeastern Bangladesh, live a number of tribal groups who are not Bengali. The most numerous are the Chakmas. Others, such as the Mros and the Tripura, are more numerous on the Indian side of the border but tend not to take too much notice of the border. They cross between the two countries quite freely through the largely jungle land that they inhabit. Many of Bangladesh's tribal people are Buddhists. Others are Hindus, Christians, or animists. Animists worship their ancestors or spirits of nature. The tribal people play little part in running the country, preferring to follow their traditional pattern of life. Even so, the tribal people in the Chittagong Hill Tract harbor considerable resentment at the way the government has encouraged Bengali people from the plains to settle in the less thickly populated hill areas. The plains people have been granted land to farm there. The government says the plains are so heavily populated, with an average of over 2,000 people living and working on every square mile of land (770 people per square kilometer) that it has to share the land fairly. It says the tribal people cannot keep all the hilly land as their own. After protests and guerrilla warfare by some of the tribal people, the government has stopped its program of resettlement.

The Biharis

Another small group of non-Bengali people in Bangladesh are known as Biharis, or sometimes "stranded Pakistanis." Although most of the 300,000 Biharis were born in Bangladesh or East Pakistan, they are the children of Muslims who left the Indian state of Bihar to settle in the eastern wing of Pakistan at partition. After the emergence of Bangladesh, they no longer felt at home in what had become a Bengali nation, and they asked to be resettled in Pakistan. Pakistan is worried that their arrival there would upset the delicate balance between different communities. There would also be a problem finding jobs for so many people. Until Pakistan agrees to take them, they will continue to live in camps in Bangladesh, lacking the rights and privileges of Bangladeshi citizens.

Pakistan's reluctance to take the Biharis is partly because of the complicated makeup of Pakistan. Although the overwhelming majority of Pakistanis are Muslims, there is very little else to hold them together. The dominant race, or ethnic group, are the Punjabis. The Punjabis are famous as one of the traditional warrior races of the subcontinent. Like Bengal, the Punjab was divided between India and Pakistan at partition. The predominantly Muslim half went to Pakistan. Hindus and Sikhs settled on the Indian side of the frontier. Punjabis from different sides

PAKISTAN AND BANGLADESH

of the frontier would expect to speak with each other in the Punjabi language. One in every three Pakistanis is a Punjabi.

The Pushtuns and the Baluchi

Another feuding, warrior race are the Pushtuns, sometimes known as the Pathans, who live along Pakistan's northwestern border with Afghanistan, as well as in Afghanistan itself. Their language is Pashto. Pushtun men wear distinctive frontier-style dress: a long, loose shirt and baggy trousers. On their heads they wear either a flat woolen hat or a vertical fez-style hat made from the woolen hide of a young lamb. Pushtuns calling themselves *mujahedin*, or holy warriors, fought inside Afghanistan against Soviet troops in the 1980s. Farther south is a large,

These villagers in northern Pakistan are Pushtuns, or Pathans. The men wear loose, baggy trousers and a distinctive flat woolen hat or a fez-style hat.

PEOPLE OF PAKISTAN AND BANGLADESH

sparsely populated region called Baluchistan. As its name suggests, it is the home of the Baluchi people. They have their own language, which is related to Pashto, and their own distinctive style of dress and life.

The Sindhi people

Karachi, the capital of the southern state of Sind, is home to the Sindhi people. That fact is the cause of one of the major sources of tension in modern Pakistan. Being a busy industrial city,

Karachi, a busy city in southern Pakistan, is home to the Sindhi people and a variety of the other peoples of Pakistan. There is rivalry between the Pushtun, Muhajir, and Sindhi people for control of the city.

Karachi has attracted many immigrants. The two largest groups to have settled there are the Pushtuns and the Muhajirs, Urdu-speaking Muslims from northern India who migrated to Pakistan at partition. There is tremendous rivalry in Karachi and nearby Hyderabad between native Sindhis, Pushtuns, and Muhajirs for control of the economy of each city and for control of the cities themselves. This rivalry has often broken out into armed warfare.

Sindhis, however, are traditionally a rural people, inhabiting and farming the southern reaches of the Indus River. The Bhutto family, who have produced two of Pakistan's prime ministers, is one of the most famous Sindhi landowning families. They come from the city of Larkana, which is located near the west bank of the Indus River in the province of Sind.

The national language
Pakistan is unusual in that hardly anyone speaks the national language, Urdu, as their mother tongue. Punjabis, Pushtuns, Sindhis, Muhajirs, and Baluchi are the main peoples of Pakistan, but there are many others, including the Kashmiris from the disputed northern territory. The only people for whom Urdu is the first language are the Muhajir settlers from northern India. Urdu is, in fact, a Persianized form of the Indian national language, Hindi. Punjabis prefer to speak Punjabi, Pushtuns speak Pashto, Baluchi speak Baluchi, and Sindhis speak Sindhi, although everyone is required to learn Urdu at school.

PEOPLE OF PAKISTAN AND BANGLADESH

The Languages of Pakistan and Bangladesh

Bengali, the language of Bangladesh and of India's West Bengal state, is written from left to right. It is based on the north Indian classical language Sanskrit. Bengali is the mother tongue of more than 150 million people. The Indian writer Rabindranath Tagore helped make the Bengali language a literary language. Many novels, poems, and plays have been written in Bengali. It is also a popular language for movies.

Urdu, the national language of Pakistan, is written from right to left. Although it is of Indian origin and closely related to the main Indian language, Hindi, Urdu has been strongly influenced by Persian. Few Pakistanis speak Urdu as their first language, but around 50 million people in India and Pakistan understand Urdu. It is considered to be the main language of Islam in the subcontinent and also has a fine literary tradition. Many poets have written in Urdu.

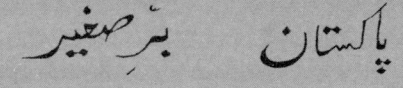

Nationalism

Some people argue that since the reason that Bangladesh broke away from Pakistan was that the Bengali language was a stronger national bond than Islam, the case for keeping together the remaining four provinces (the Punjab, Sind, Baluchistan, and North-West Frontier Province) under the umbrella of Pakistan has weakened. They consider Urdu to be an artificial language promoted to hold Pakistan together rather than a real common bond between the various peoples. A person from the North-West Frontier Province, for example, probably thinks of himself as a Pushtun first and a Muslim second, which makes him question why he should be part of a nation that was founded on a religious rather than a language basis. This feeling of nationalism among Sindhis, Baluchi, and Pushtuns has led their leaders to call for more autonomy, or control, of their own affairs. None of them likes the feeling that they are dominated by the Punjabis, who tend to be strong in government and who also control the army.

6 The Way of Life

The different peoples who live in Pakistan and Bangladesh all have their own customs and traditions. Those living on the plains inevitably have a different life-style from those living in mountainous regions. Even so, in many ways the life-styles of the different peoples who make up Pakistan, Bangladesh, and their neighbor India are very similar. Most Pakistanis or Bangladeshis are poor, and their way of life reflects this poverty. As in any country, there are some very wealthy people, too.

Standards of living

The biggest difference in standards of living is between those who live in the cities and those

The majority of Bangladeshis live in rural areas. Their homes are usually very simple. Cooking is often done outdoors, and they may have to fetch water from a river or a stream.

who live in the countryside. Around 78 percent of Bangladeshis and 68 percent of Pakistanis live in the countryside. In Bangladesh the majority of the city dwellers live in the capital, Dacca, or in the two port cities, Chittagong and Khulna. In Pakistan the main centers of population are the cities of Karachi and Lahore. People who live in the cities generally have the benefit of better-quality homes, probably with running water and electricity. Many have jobs and travel to work by cycle rickshaw, motorized rickshaw or bus, or perhaps by bicycle. Some even own a car.

In the cities of both Pakistan and Bangladesh, the usual practice is for the women to stay at home and care for the house, preparing food for

Dacca—Bangladesh's Capital
Dacca became capital of the new nation of Bangladesh in 1971. It is situated on the banks of the Padma River. It first became the capital city of Bengal during Mogul rule, but Calcutta, now the capital of the Indian state of West Bengal, was the more important city until partition. Dacca seems like a new city, one in which the modern art of town planning has been applied. The main government buildings, including the parliament building, have all been constructed in the past 40 years. Dacca has become quite an industrial city. It has a business district, called Motijeel, as well as a famous university. The area around Dacca is so low-lying that when the floods come, Dacca appears to be virtually cut off from the surrounding countryside. About 4 million people live in Dacca, one of the most densely populated parts of the country.

the men when they return from work. The women go to market to buy the food. They probably look after the household finances, too. Food is generally cooked on a modern gas stove or in an electric oven. A wealthy household usually possesses a refrigerator, a very useful appliance in hot countries like Bangladesh and Pakistan. Without a refrigerator it is necessary to buy fresh food every day.

Nearly everything is available to those who live in the city. The markets contain a wide selection of locally grown produce as well as goods brought

---

Islamabad—Pakistan's Capital

When Pakistan separated from India in 1947, its leaders decided to build a new capital city, which they called Islamabad after the religion that had given rise to the creation of Pakistan. It was many years before construction began. At first Karachi, the main seaport and largest city, was Pakistan's capital. Later Rawalpindi became the capital. Islamabad was carefully planned and laid out next to Rawalpindi at the point where the mountains give way to the plains. The two cities share the international airport, which is situated between them. Islamabad is in fact still under construction and is likely to be so for many years. However, the main government buildings have all been completed. They include the parliament building, the president's house, and the main secretariat, as well as the Shah Faisal Mosque. A university has also been established in the city. Although it covers a large area, fewer than half a million people live in Islamabad. The city is divided into zones, and each street has a number.

from farther away, even from abroad. However, the cost of goods is higher in the city than in the countryside. City life is more costly but is generally more comfortable, too. In their spare time, city dwellers like to meet friends for a drink, play sports, or go to one of the many movie theaters to watch a film.

Islamabad, the capital of Pakistan, is a new, carefully planned city.

THE WAY OF LIFE

Large cities such as Dacca have modern offices and apartment buildings such as those pictured. These buildings have all the facilities needed for an up-to-date life-style.

The lure of the city

There is another side to city life. The bright lights and entertainment, as well as the greater opportunities for finding work, attract people to the city. This is especially true of Bangladesh, where it is difficult to make a living in the countryside because there are so many people. At first, those who migrate to the city can expect to live in a shantytown on the outskirts of town. The shantytowns, or slums, are without running water and toilet facilities, and certainly without electricity. But people are willing to endure this discomfort in return for the better employment prospects in the city.

Often a man leaves his family in the village and travels to the big city to find work. He may try to become a rickshaw driver. To do this he leases his rickshaw on a daily basis, and he starts to earn money for himself only when he has made enough money to pay the rental fee. The high number of rickshaw "wallahs," as they are called, competing for passengers makes earning a living this way very hard work. Still, the man hopes to earn enough to be able to send some back to his family in the village. The rickshaw wallahs, incidentally, usually sleep in their rickshaws, which solves the problem of accommodations—at least until it rains.

Village life
Back in the village the rickshaw wallah's family lives a very different life-style. They probably live in a home made of wood, cane, and possibly mud. It is unlikely to be built of brick or cement. The houses in a typical village do not have running water. Water must be carried from a well or a pump, possibly some distance away. The fields or wasteland provide toilets, which people use in the early morning or after dark so that they can have some privacy. Bangladesh's rural population is spread evenly across the land. The very heavy density of population means that wherever you go in the country there are people in view. They may be tending the field or their animals, or simply walking along the street. Pakistan's rural population is concentrated largely in the east of the country on land nourished by the Indus River and its tributaries. Away from the river, large areas of the country are uninhabitable.

As in the cities, women in the villages do the shopping and cooking. In rural areas, cooking is more likely to be done over a wood fire or kerosene stove. There are wide variations in diet.

THE WAY OF LIFE

Food

Pakistanis tend to be meat eaters. The Punjabis and Pushtuns, in particular, consume a great deal of meat. This may be from the cow, buffalo, or goat but never from the pig, an animal considered to be unclean by Muslims. Chicken is also popular in both Pakistan and Bangladesh.

Pakistanis eat a lot of wheat, usually baked into a bread called *nan* or into *chapatty*, which are unleavened (made without yeast), so they are like flat rolls. Rice, of course, is eaten in both countries, and a lot of Pakistani rice is sold abroad. Vegetables are popular because they are nutritious and cheaper than meat, but their availability depends on the region and the seasons. The central market in a city like Dacca or Lahore would always have a good supply of vegetables.

Fruits that are popular in both countries include the large, sweet jackfruit, mango, papaya, orange, banana, and pineapple. Dates grow in some areas of Pakistan. Alcohol consumption is forbidden under the religious laws of both countries. Favorite drinks are carbonated or are made from fruit juice.

In a market in a large city a wide range of food is always available. This stall in a Pakistani city is selling beans, lentils, and a variety of nuts. These are widely used in Pakistani cooking.

55

Bangladeshis are rice eaters, and the most popular supplement to the basic bowl of rice is fish caught either in the river or offshore in the Bay of Bengal. A Bangladeshi freshwater delicacy is the smoked hilsa fish. There is a growing industry, too, in breeding fish and shrimps in the water-logged rice fields, although the shrimps produced in this way are mainly exported. Fish is the major source of protein in Bangladesh.

Muslim customs
Muslim customs affect every aspect of life. It is usual for women to remain in purdah, covered from the gaze of men who are not their husbands, but the extent to which this is observed varies from region to region. In the North-West Frontier Province of Pakistan it is very rare to see a woman in the streets uncovered and somewhat unusual to see women out at all. Peshawar, the capital city of the province, seems to be a man's city. The women stay at home while the men go to work in the fields tending their wheat, rice, or vegetables and carrying their produce to sell at the market. Yet in the cotton-growing region of the Punjab Province, it is the women who traditionally pick the cotton. It is the men who can be seen turning toward the Arabian city of Mecca to do their *puja*, or say their prayers, at set times of the day. On Fridays, the holy day in both countries, the men go the mosque to pray. Mosques are found in towns and villages throughout Bangladesh and Pakistan. Big mosques in the cities are very crowded on Fridays.

Marriages are usually arranged between the families of the bride and bridegroom, who

THE WAY OF LIFE

This Bengali bride is having her hands decorated as part of the traditional marriage celebration.

probably have very little choice in the matter. They are content to follow the guidance of their parents in keeping with tradition. A marriage, which is generally blessed in the mosque, is an occasion for a great feast to which lots of people are invited. Muslim law allows a man to marry up to four wives, although he has to treat each wife equally. Many men are content to have just one wife. This is just as well, or there would be a shortage of prospective brides!

7 Farming and Fishing

Both Pakistan and Bangladesh are essentially rural countries, and the majority of their people live and work in the countryside. Their main activity is farming—producing and processing the grain and other foodstuffs that they need to survive. In Pakistan more than half of all families are directly dependent on farming. In Bangladesh probably as many as 85 percent are farmers or fishermen. Both countries grow a great deal of rice in wet paddy-field cultivation.

For Pakistan, wheat is as important as rice. However, whereas Pakistan as a nation is able to feed itself and has rice left for export, Bangladesh, with its much smaller land area, finds it difficult to produce enough rice to meet the needs of its own population.

Planting rice in Bangladeshi rice paddies is a backbreaking task. More than 26 million acres (10.5 million hectares) of land is devoted to rice growing in Bangladesh.

THE WAY OF LIFE

Famine and flood

Bangladesh struggles constantly to produce enough food for its people. The problem, of course, is that there are so many people. The country supports more than 110 million people,

---

Bangladesh—A Nation under Water
Bangladesh is the last stop on the route taken by the southwestern monsoon rains that make their way up from southern India during June and July each year. Parts of the northeast of the country around Sylhet receive more than 200 inches (500 centimeters) annually. There are two other reasons why Bangladesh receives so much water, which usually results in flooding. The melting of the Himalayan snows during the summer months adds quickly to the amount of water flowing through the country's rivers. Also, the unusual weather that comes with the monsoon rains creates strong winds that can have a terrible effect when they blow onshore, making tidal waves that flood low-lying areas with seawater. Sometimes these cyclones cause a heavy loss of life. As many as half a million people were drowned in 1970, and another disastrous cyclone in 1991 killed about 150,000 people. The result of all these problems is that Bangladesh fights an annual struggle to remain above water and at the same time to grow enough crops to feed its people. Bangladesh in the rainy season is a nation that is barely visible above water. Its 110 million people crowd into the cities, onto the roadsides and railroad embankments, and any other relatively high ground as the waters rise. Water is both the country's greatest natural resource and its worst enemy.

PAKISTAN AND BANGLADESH

and the population is growing all the time.

Historically Bengal has suffered many famines, when it has been unable to feed all its people. This may have been because the monsoon rains failed to materialize or did not last as long as expected, or because heavy flooding destroyed crops. There was a terrible famine in 1943 when as many as half a million people starved to death. Today if the monsoon fails, other nations swiftly provide emergency food rations. Bangladesh would, of course, like to be able to feed all its people without depending on foreign help, and it has tried to become self-sufficient in rice production. In some

Many areas of Pakistan have little rainfall. Rivers fed with water from the mountains are now being used to help irrigate the land. The increased use of chemical fertilizers is also helping to produce more crops. This farmer in Baluchistan is still using the traditional ox plow to break up his soil.

FARMING AND FISHING

years it has reached this target, but in bad years self-sufficiency is still out of reach.

Water is the lifeblood of both Bangladesh and Pakistan. Bangladesh often seems to have too much of it falling from the sky during the rainy seasons and bursting the banks of its many rivers. But, if there were any less rainfall, Bangladesh would not be able to harvest the three crops a year that its fertile soil allows in some areas. Annually Bangladesh produces more than enough rice to feed all the people of even a large European nation, like France and Germany. Nevertheless even this much rice may not suffice for this populous nation.

Pakistan, by contrast, has too little rain in some areas and must depend on irrigation to supply water in dry places. Extending irrigation has enabled Pakistan to expand significantly the area of land on which it can grow crops. The use of chemical fertilizers and high-yielding varieties of wheat has considerably increased its production of wheat in recent years, although this amount still tends to fall slightly short of its needs.

Besides their basic food grains, Pakistan and Bangladesh each have an important cash crop that is equally dependent on water. In Pakistan that crop is cotton. It is the single most important crop for the Pakistani economy and is responsible for more than a third of what the country earns from exports.

Pakistan's next most important agricultural product is sugarcane. Sugarcane grows in the same type of soil as cotton. Many farmers have switched from cotton to sugarcane, finding it to be more profitable.

"The golden fiber"

In Bangladesh the key cash crop is jute, a tall fibrous plant used to make rope, sacking, and the backing of carpets. Small farmers often grow clumps of jute at the edge of their rice paddies so that no matter how the rice fares, they have something to sell for cash. Jute is so valuable to ordinary farmers as a source of income that they call it "the golden fiber." Although jute remains an important source of export earnings for Bangladesh, its importance has declined somewhat as the country has developed other small-scale industries, such as textiles and leather products.

After jute, another important Bangladeshi crop is tea, which is grown in the gardens around Sylhet in the eastern part of the country. Many British and American tea companies buy their tea leaves from Bangladesh or from the adjoining tea gardens of Assam in northeastern India. Other crops grown include lentils, beans and other edible seeds, corn for animal feed, edible oilseed, tobacco, and citrus and other tropical fruits.

Recently Bangladesh has developed an interesting new industry—shrimp farming. Rice farmers use some of their land to cultivate these freshwater creatures, more or less as a sideline to rice farming. Most of the shrimps are then frozen and flown to a very appreciative market in Japan. Few Bangladeshis benefit from these fish products, although they do provide a valuable source of foreign currency, which can in turn, be used to buy machinery, oil, and many of the other things that Bangladesh needs but cannot produce for itself.

FARMING AND FISHING

Tea is a major cash crop in Bangladesh, which is the fifth largest producer and exporter of tea in the world. These women are picking tea leaves in the Chittagong Hill Tracts, where the soil and climate are ideal for tea growing.

International aid

The products produced by farmers and fishermen should be enough to provide a nutritious and well-balanced diet for all Bangladeshis and Pakistanis. Yet, the problem in these countries that have such large populations, especially Bangladesh, is ensuring that there is enough food to go around.

To ensure adequate food for the population, international aid organizations, including the U.N. Food and Agricultural Organization and the World Food Program, have large and active development projects in Bangladesh. Not many countries have soil as fertile as that of Bangladesh, capable of producing up to three crops a year. The challenge for Bangladesh is to

PAKISTAN AND BANGLADESH

The numerous rivers, streams, lakes, and ponds of Bangladesh provide fish, an important part of the Bangladeshi diet. These villagers are using a traditional method of netting fish.

follow the examples of India, Pakistan, and other Asian nations in improving the efficiency of farming techniques to provide enough food to go around. Many experts believe that becoming truly self-sufficient in rice production is the key to breaking the cycle of poverty in Bangladesh. The most important difference between the people of Pakistan and Bangladesh is that in Pakistan people do not go hungry, whereas Bangladesh often depends on massive imports of grain to ensure that nobody starves.

8 Industry, Trade, and Energy

Both Bangladesh and Pakistan are agricultural countries whose main products are grown rather than made. Neither country is primarily an industrial nation, although both have ambitions to develop their industry so that they are no longer so dependent on what they grow. Both have taken steps in this direction by processing into goods the things they grow. Pakistan now exports less raw cotton but more goods made out of cotton, and the wool from its sheep is made into carpets. Carpet making is a traditional family skill in parts of the north, especially Kashmir, where several members of the same family do the weaving together. It may take several months to produce one carpet. It is a skill that is passed down from one generation to the next.

Other industries

Other growing industries in Pakistan are the processing of tobacco and sugar, papermaking, and the making of animal hides into leather goods. Some secondary industries include the manufacture of fertilizers for farming; consumer goods, including some electrical appliances; and cement and steel making. The country has deposits of several important minerals, such as copper, iron ore used in steel making, and limestone for the cement industry. There is also an industry assembling imported car and truck parts, and several factories making tractors.

PAKISTAN AND BANGLADESH

Pakistan produces more than 7 million tons of cement each year, using limestone that has been mined in the country. This large cement works is near the city of Hyderabad.

Tractors are gradually replacing bullocks for pulling plows in the fields. Sporting goods, such as soccer balls, hockey sticks, and cricket bats, are made and sold abroad.

Energy for industry

Much of Pakistan's heavy industry is centered in Karachi, the country's major city and only port. Natural gas has been found at Sui in the south of the country, and pipelines have been built to carry gas to Karachi and other cities, where it is used to fuel factories and homes. Pakistan also has coal deposits as well as small reserves of oil, although not enough to satisfy its needs. Pakistan is making use of the mountainous terrain in the north of the country to provide hydroelectric

INDUSTRY, TRADE, AND ENERGY

> **The Tarbela Dam**
> The Tarbela Dam, on the Indus River, is the largest rock-filled dam in the world, larger than the Aswan Dam on the Nile in Egypt. It is situated in Pakistan at the point where the Indus River emerges from the hills onto the plains, not far from the capital, Islamabad. After Pakistan reached an agreement with India as to how the waters of this important river were to be shared between the two countries, Pakistan started work on this massive hydroelectricity engineering project with the financial help of the World Bank. The dam was completed in 1975. The Tarbela Dam is 486 feet (148 meters) high, measures 1.7 miles (2.7 kilometers) across the top, and has led to the formation of a lake that is 19 miles (30 kilometers) long and can hold 180 million cubic yards (140 million cubic meters) of water. During the summer, when the mountain snows are melting, the water crossing the dam's spillway makes a spectacular sight—rushing down and then leaping into the air like a monumental fountain. Visitors are sometimes allowed to drive across the rim of the dam. Tarbela's turbines generate 1,750 megawatts of electricity, providing a large proportion of the country's electricity needs.

power. Energy needs are growing so fast that Pakistan is also developing nuclear energy.

Bangladeshi exports
Where once Bangladesh sold abroad only primary products, such as tea and jute, it has now developed its textile industry and is selling finished garments abroad. Textiles are now a

PAKISTAN AND BANGLADESH

Cotton growing and cotton weaving are major industries in Bangladesh. Although there are large factories making textiles, weaving is also an important cottage industry. It provides work in many rural areas.

more important export than jute. But, because Bangladesh does not produce enough cotton and other yarn to manufacture garments, it must import these raw materials.

In developing its textile industry, Bangladesh is making use of "cheap labor." Its people are paid less to work in clothing factories than they would be in a wealthier country. For this reason, Bangladeshi factories can produce items of clothing more cheaply than a richer country can. Bangladesh is also trying to process its jute into carpet backing, which earns more money than the sale of the raw fibers. Like Pakistan, Bangladesh is competing to sell leather shoes and jackets abroad rather than simply leather.

Other agricultural products that are processed

INDUSTRY, TRADE, AND ENERGY

Here raw jute is being prepared for export. Bangladesh produces about 70 percent of the world's raw jute. Although it is the highest earning of Bangladesh's exports, ways of processing jute into products for export are being developed because this would be more profitable.

into finished goods are tea and timber. Tea is dried, processed, and packaged before being exported. Some of the trees from the Sundarbans provide very good newsprint, the paper on which newspapers are printed. Bangladesh has a thriving newsprint industry, enough to supply its own newspapers and to sell to other countries. Sugar is refined in sugar factories. Jute fiber, leather, and other agricultural products are also used in handicraft industries, such as the making of carpets, leather purses, and wallets as well as cane furniture. These industries are based at home or in small village factories. Such enterprises are usually owned by a single family, whose members help in the manufacturing process.

PAKISTAN AND BANGLADESH

The Teesta barrage is part of a massive irrigation project in northwestern Bangladesh. Both Pakistan and Bangladesh are aware of the need to create power for their expanding industries. They are developing ways of harnessing their abundant water supplies to make hydroelectricity.

Heavy industry

Bangladesh also has some heavy industry, including a steel foundry at Chittagong, an aluminum smelter and some cement works, and a small shipyard. None of these can cope with the country's own needs for the products of these industries, so it also has to import such things, paying for them with the money earned by selling jute, tea, and clothing abroad. Bangladesh would very much like to build bigger and better factories to make more of the products it needs. One of its main problems is a shortage of technical skills. Another is a shortage of fuel with which to power its factories.

Bangladesh does have some natural gas, and small quantities of oil have recently been discovered, but neither occurs in sufficient

INDUSTRY, TRADE, AND ENERGY

quantities to be of much use to the country's development. There are also reserves of coal and lignite, a soft brown type of coal but again only in small quantities. Also, a small amount of uranium has been found but not enough for the country to think of developing nuclear energy.

For a country with so much water, little of it is put to work to provide power for factories and homes. The main hydroelectric plant is in the Chittagong Hill Tracts in southeast Bangladesh. If the waters of the Padma River and other rivers were harnessed, they could generate a great deal of electricity. Bangladesh is regarded by the rest of the world as a country that has few resources of its own (except people). If its water could be put to good use, it could become a relatively well-off country. Also, if it did not have to concentrate its efforts to such an extent on growing food for its rising population, more attention might be devoted to searching for mineral deposits. It is possible that Bangladesh is much richer in oil and other minerals than anyone has so far realized.

9 Transportation and Communications

Most people visiting Pakistan these days arrive by air. It is surprising that Pakistan, which has been invaded many times throughout history, has only limited access routes by road. This is partly because strained relations with neighbors India and Afghanistan have caused borders to be closed. The other reason is the huge natural obstacle formed by the mountains that guard the northern approaches to Pakistan.

The gateway to India
Four main land routes link Pakistan to four different countries. Two of these are engineering marvels. One, the Khyber Pass, which links Pakistan and Afghanistan, became famous because it marked the western extremity of British colonial rule in India. Even today the area around Khyber is renowned for the way in which its tribal inhabitants have resisted being brought under the control of the government in Islamabad. It was the main gateway through which the Aryans and other invaders from Arabia, Turkey, and Persia arrived on the Indian subcontinent. From the Afghan border post at Torkham, the road passes through barren country to a high point of 3,517 feet (1,072 meters) before descending again. Following the road past many abandoned forts, the traveler eventually arrives at the Pakistani frontier town of Peshawar.

Although it is several centuries newer, the

TRANSPORTATION AND COMMUNICATIONS

The road through the Khyber Pass, which links Pakistan and Afghanistan, twists and turns between high mountains. This road, with its tunnels carved through rock, is a major engineering feat.

Karakoram Highway, which threads its way 805 miles (1,300 kilometers) from Islamabad through the Karakoram Mountains to cross into China near the city of Kashgar, is one of the engineering wonders of the modern world. It was started in 1959 as a joint project between the Pakistani and Chinese governments and was completed nearly 20 years later. Following the path of the old Silk Road to China, the Karakoram Highway rises to a

PAKISTAN AND BANGLADESH

high point of 15,528 feet (4,733 meters) at the Karakoram Pass where it enters China. It takes three or four days to cover the entire journey to Kashgar. Rock falls, landslides, and the movement of glaciers mean the highway requires constant maintenance.

A third long-distance route connects Pakistan to Iran across the wilderness of Baluchistan. A traveler leaving the city of Quetta in western Pakistan will arrive many hours later at the southern Iranian city of Zahedan, having risked sandstorms and the ever-present danger of being robbed by the bandits who live in Baluchistan. The main road into Pakistan from India connects the city of Amritsar in India to that of Lahore in Pakistan. Both cities were part of undivided Punjab before partition. The journey takes less

A traditional method of transportation, the bullock cart, vies for space with motorized traffic in this busy street in Lahore.

than two hours, but the prevailing hostility between the two neighbors means that the few travelers allowed to make the trip can expect to encounter at least another two hours of interrogation by immigration and customs officials at the border. The road forms part of the Grand Trunk Road, which once linked Peshawar with Calcutta, the capital of Bengal.

Roads and railroads in Pakistan
Since the partition of the subcontinent, Pakistanis consider that the Grand Trunk Road now connects Peshawar, on the northwestern frontier, to Karachi, the main industrial city and port. This route of 1,080 miles (1,740 kilometers) is the main road in a network of paved roads and highways that extends for 37,300 miles (60,000 kilometers) into all corners of the country. Colorful trucks and buses travel between towns, although the low standards of driving and vehicle maintenance mean that buses and trucks commonly break down or run into a ditch at the roadside, often with heavy loss of life or injury because buses are invariably overcrowded. People even travel on the roof if the bus is filled!

Railroads are a cheap and popular means of transportation as well as the main means of transporting freight. Railroad lines connect all the main cities. Main lines connect the provincial capitals of Karachi, Quetta, Peshawar, and Lahore. The railroads are part of the elaborate system built by the British, and lines still connect across the border into the Indian railroad system. (Travel on these routes is restricted.) The only areas of Pakistan not reached by the railroad

PAKISTAN AND BANGLADESH

Railroads are a popular method of transportation in both Pakistan and Bangladesh. The railroad system was built during British rule. The vendor in this photograph is selling food to passengers on the Awam Express at Rawalpindi, Pakistan.

network are the northern, mountainous areas. Here, the only way to avoid twisty roads at risk from landslides is to fly by small aircraft.

Going by boat

The most important means of transportation in Bangladesh is by river. There are aout 5,240 miles (8,433 kilometers) of navigable waterways, compared with less than 2,000 miles (3,000 kilometers) of railroad. So many rivers crisscross the country that travel by river is often the quickest way of traveling between two places. Because of a shortage of bridges, motorized ferries are used to transport vehicles and pedestrians from one bank to another, while manpowered boats transport passengers across

TRANSPORTATION AND COMMUNICATIONS

Travel by Air

Pakistan International Airlines (PIA) flies between 32 towns and cities around the country, including many small towns in the mountainous region where there is barely room for a runway. Flights once or twice a day by small aircraft to Gilgit, Hunza, and Swat connect these previously isolated hill valleys to Islamabad. Regular flights several times a day connect the major cities of Karachi, Lahore, Peshawar, Quetta, and Islamabad (which shares an airport with Rawalpindi). With its fleet of Boeings and airbuses, PIA also connects Pakistan with 41 cities abroad, including Tokyo, New York, Toronto, and London. There are frequent flights to the Persian Gulf region, catering to the large number of Pakistanis who go there to work, as well as to the holy cities of Saudi Arabia, for Muslim pilgrims. Karachi is the main international airport.

Bangladesh Biman, the national airline of Bangladesh, flies regular flights between the main cities of Dacca, Chittagong, Jessore, Sylhet, Rajshahi, Saidpur, and Cox's Bazar. It also serves 26 overseas destinations, including London and Paris, mainly with its wide-bodied DC-10s. Many international airlines fly into Dacca.

smaller rivers for a small fee. Small boats are also the main means of transporting produce to market. Barisol, Chalna Port, Chandpur, Dacca, and Narayanganj are major river ports. Passenger steamers and ferries on the rivers are often overloaded and sit low in the water. During the monsoon season, steamers often sink, making it a risky form of travel.

PAKISTAN AND BANGLADESH

Train travel in Bangladesh

Bangladeshi railroads were also built by the British. Some passengers travel on the roofs of railroad cars to avoid paying their fare, or because there is no room inside. Yet, train travel is cheap, even by local standards. The railroad system is owned and operated by the government. During the monsoon season when the land floods, railroad tracks can be washed away or embankments can become unsafe. The network of roads also falls victim to flooding and needs frequent repair, even though the roads and railroads have been built on embankments. Because Bangladesh has so little high ground, when the floods come, people take refuge from their flooded homes along the road and railroad embankments.

All forms of transportation can get very crowded! It is quite usual to see buses in either country with passengers not only riding on the roof but clinging to the back and sides—wherever they can gain a foothold.

10 Health, Education, and Welfare

Waterborne diseases are the major health hazard in Bangladesh. Dirty water is the major cause of disease, and epidemics are especially likely to break out during the rainy season. In the cities the cramped and unsanitary housing conditions cause similar problems. Diarrhea is such a problem that Bangladesh has a center for the study of its causes. The center tries to find ways to prevent it. Diarrhea can be a fatal disease in Bangladesh, especially among children, because it leads to dehydration. Other diseases that are common in Bangladesh and are spread through water are malaria and cholera. Large-scale spraying of ponds and lakes takes place regularly to try to prevent the malaria-carrying mosquito from breeding in the water.

Health care in Bangladesh
In Bangladesh the standard of health is low, diseases are widespread, and there is not an adequate supply of doctors or medical workers. Due to poor health and inadequate diet, most Bangladeshis do not live as long as most people in developed countries. The government tries to improve health care, and plenty of doctors are being trained in the country's seven medical schools. Unfortunately, however, many medical students go abroad for further training and then decide not to return home. This benefits their adopted country, but it does not help improve

PAKISTAN AND BANGLADESH

The standard of health is low in Bangladesh. The government is encouraging immunization against many of the tropical diseases, such as malaria, cholera, and tuberculosis, that kill so many Bangladeshis.

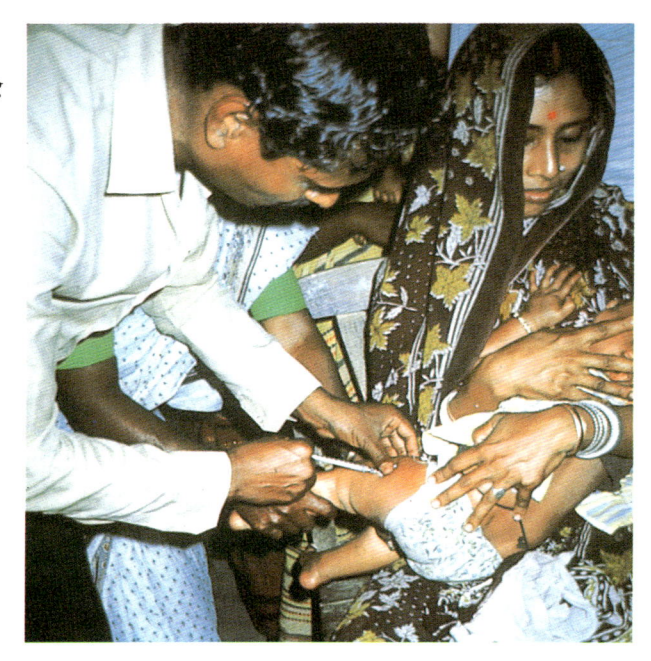

medical care back in Bangladesh. As part of its program to improve the standards of health, hygiene, and sanitation, the government also encourages people to try to limit the size of their families. They are well aware that the faster the population grows, the less care, and indeed food, each person gets and the more cramped living conditions become. Tuberculosis, a disease of the lungs, is common as a result of cramped living conditions. Trying to stop population growth is a major goal of the government.

Education in Bangladesh
Although schooling in Bangladesh is free for all children, many of them do not go to school

HEALTH, EDUCATION, AND WELFARE

In both countries, children in rural areas often do not go to school, but in the cities the attendance is much higher. These girls in a city school in Bangladesh have to work in a very crowded classroom. As it is a Muslim country, they are taught separately from the boys.

because they are needed to help their parents in the fields. As a result, about half of all children grow up unable to read and write. Among the wealthier families, however, education is regarded very highly. Children are encouraged to complete their schooling and then go on for further studies at one of the many universities and colleges of higher education around the country. Some colleges concentrate on farming skills, others on engineering, while others offer a whole range of subjects. There are also teacher-training colleges. The best-known institute of learning in the country is the University of Dacca. It teaches a wide range of subjects, including law, economics, and journalism.

Students from the University of Dacca have often gone on strike or demonstrated on the streets of the capital when they were unhappy about the political situation. The students played an important role in forcing former president Ershad to resign. Student protest is a tradition among Bengalis. Across the border in Indian West Bengal, students at Calcutta University, one of the largest in the world, believe they virtually invented student protest. Long before students in the United States or Europe joined together in the late 1960s to demonstrate against the actions of their governments, the students at Calcutta were protesting the actions of their government.

Pakistan's health problems
Pakistan has different health problems than Bangladesh, although its problems often derive also from unsanitary living conditions and lack of basic hygiene. Malnutrition, or poor diet, is a problem among children, possibly because families tend to be large, and there may not be enough food to go around. Diseases that can easily be prevented and almost as easily cured these days—such as tuberculosis and leprosy—are still common in Pakistan. They exist because uneducated people have not learned how to avoid contracting such diseases and because medical care is lacking. Only in the big cities are there good hospitals, and poor people generally do not consult doctors because they cannot pay for medical care.

Some people complain that Pakistan has spent too much on building up its army and not enough on health care and disease prevention. Spending more money on bringing drinking water to homes would instantly improve public health because many diseases result from unsanitary washing and eating conditions. United Nations agencies have helped carry out immunization programs to protect children against diseases such as diphtheria, tuberculosis, polio, and measles.

A growing problem in Pakistan's cities is drug addiction. The availability of opium, which is grown in the North-West Frontier Province and across the border in Afghanistan, has become a major social problem, especially in the city of Karachi. Drug traffickers have become very rich and powerful by selling drugs abroad as well as to Pakistanis.

Education in Pakistan
About 75 percent of all Pakistanis cannot read and write. School education and literacy programs have been neglected, although efforts are now underway to improve education for all. Many more women than men are unable to read and write. In rural areas, many children do not go to school. As soon as they are old enough, they accompany their mother or father to work in the fields.

It is perhaps surprising, given the low standard of school education, that Pakistan is very proud of its tradition of higher education, which has produced doctors, scientists, and engineers who are among the best in the world. All major cities have at least one university. The oldest is the University of Punjab in Lahore, which was founded more than a hundred years ago.

Women tend to be much less educated than men in rural areas because their role in life is

PAKISTAN AND BANGLADESH

The University of Punjab in Lahore is one of 22 universities in Pakistan. There are about 130,000 students at universities and colleges in Pakistan, but only about 20,000 of these are women. Fewer women go into higher education because the Muslim religion teaches that women should stay at home.

considered to be that of keeping house and bringing up children for which education is not thought to be necessary. Such attitudes have virtually disappeared from the major cities as a result of exposure through television to Western attitudes. Young women are well represented at universities and colleges. The fact that Pakistan and Bangladesh have recently had women prime ministers shows that fewer jobs are barred to women these days.

11 Sports, Leisure, and the Arts

Two sports, cricket and field hockey, are played in Pakistan with great enthusiasm. In both, Pakistanis have proved themselves to be among the best in the world. The cricketer Imran Khan is particularly well known. In the North-West Frontier Province, a form of polo is played. The game of polo, in which players hit a ball while riding on horseback, originated in Persia (present-day Iran) and was introduced to the subcontinent by the Moguls. Polo was a popular sport during British rule, especially among army officers. It was introduced to the United States and Britain by India. The version of the game that is popular among Pushtuns uses the headless carcass of a goat instead of a ball and is called *buzkashi*. Squash is also popular. A Pushtun, Jehangir Khan, has been world squash champion for a record number of times.

Cricket is played in Bangladesh but not with the same enthusiasm as in India, Pakistan, and Sri Lanka. Bangladeshis prefer soccer and field hockey. A popular traditional game is *ha-do-do*, a game of "catch" of sorts played between opposing teams trying to capture each other's territory.

Several indoor games that are popular in Western countries are played in Pakistan and Bangladesh. They include chess and card games, especially bridge. Hunting and wrestling are two other popular leisure activities in Pakistan.

PAKISTAN AND BANGLADESH

The Pakistanis have dominated international squash since the late 1970s. Jehangir Khan, a Pushtun, has been world squash champion many times.

The arts

Bangladesh shares the musical and dramatic tradition of Indian Bengal. The sitar, a stringed instrument, is played by skilled professional musicians. The Bengali language is a very rich one that has given rise to a lot of writing including stories, plays, and poetry. Plays are often performed by theater groups. There is also a famous Bangladeshi painting tradition. Zainul Abedin is one of the country's best-known painters.

SPORTS, LEISURE, AND THE ARTS

Movies are a very important form of entertainment in both Pakistan and Bangladesh. These movie posters in a bazaar in Peshawar, Pakistan, are advertising the latest adventure epic. Films are made in all the countries of the subcontinent.

The Movies
The most popular form of entertainment in Pakistan and Bangladesh is the movies. Even fairly small towns have a movie house where films made in Pakistan, India, and Bangladesh are shown. India makes more films than any other country in the world, but Pakistan and Bangladesh also have thriving film industries. About 60 films are produced each year in Bangladesh alone. There are always large and enthusiastic audiences to watch the films. One reason why the movies are so popular is that few people can afford to buy a television set. However, even in cities where television is becoming commonplace, young people still enjoy packing the city's movie theater to watch the latest love story starring well-known actors and actresses. Most films are musicals. Often the songs from such films become hit tunes among moviegoers.

PAKISTAN AND BANGLADESH

In Bangladesh there are a number of music and drama groups who play traditional music and recount stories of myths and legends.

Pakistan's cultural tradition is much more diverse because not many people speak Urdu as their first language. Punjabis tend to have one cultural tradition while Sindhis, Baluchi, and Pushtuns have their own. Music, song, and dance play a key part in Pakistani culture, and both Pakistanis and Bangladeshis love music. In a cross-country bus, it is not unusual for the driver to put on his radio or cassette player before beginning the journey. People enjoy hearing the latest musical hits.

Architecture

One way in which the culture of different peoples finds expression is in architecture. Both countries have followed Islamic tradition, building their mosques and other buildings according to religious teachings. At the same time they have Pakistani or Bangladeshi characteristics. The Badshahi Mosque in Lahore, which was built by the Moguls, is one of the finest and largest in the world and has tall minarets at each of its four corners. The grand Shah Faisal Mosque in Islamabad is considerably more modern in design but has incorporated traditional Pakistani patterns. Dacca's grandest mosque is called Baitul Mukarram. It is one of an estimated 800 mosques in the capital city. Both Pakistan and Bangladesh have modern parliament buildings, reflecting the fact that both are young countries. However, there are also many older buildings that were built during the British period of rule or earlier.

12 Pakistan and Bangladesh Today

Pakistan and Bangladesh are traditional societies faced with the difficulties of adjusting to a modern world. Since the end of British rule in 1947, the biggest problem has been establishing their own system of government—both as one country and then, after 1971, as separate countries. Both have been ruled by the army for more than half of the time they have been independent nations as a result of military leaders overthrowing the elected political leaders. On the whole the people have not liked being ruled by the army, so they have demonstrated against

In large cities more women now work outside the home in spite of pressure from the strict observers of Islam. Like these Bangladeshi women, they often work alongside men.

military rule, demanding that civilian politicians be freed from prison and allowed to take part in elections once more. Often this has happened, only to have the army take power again a few years later. Trying to develop effective democratic political institutions in which the ordinary people decide who is to form their governments has been the biggest challenge facing the people of Pakistan and Bangladesh.

Religion and government
Another challenge has come from the dominant religion, Islam. There has been a trend in the Middle East, best demonstrated by Iran, for religion and religious leaders to play a strong role in government. In Iran, for example, many people want the country to be run along religious lines and for Islamic law to take precedence over the law passed by parliament. Pakistan, including what is now Bangladesh, broke away from India because it did not want to be dominated by Hindu leaders. Muslims wanted a nation of their own. Yet many Muslims believe that even though most of the people are Muslims, religion should be kept out of government. They believe that the country should be run by elected leaders who should make laws in parliament according to the needs of the moment. The debate about whether Pakistan and Bangladesh should become Muslim states instead of secular states raged throughout the 1980s. Some leaders, like General Zia-ul-Haq of Pakistan and General Ershad of Bangladesh, believed in strengthening their country's links with Muslim countries in the Middle East.

PAKISTAN AND BANGLADESH

Flooding is a major hazard in Bangladesh during the monsoon and is one of the most important problems the government needs to tackle before it can improve the country's economy.

The debate about the place of religion affects the ordinary citizen, too. Should women stay in the home and cover themselves from head to foot when they go to market, or should they change with the times and, like women in the West, play a full role in society? This is a controversial question. Many people feel strongly that women should observe purdah; others believe equally strongly that women should not be treated as second-class citizens, which is how they regard the observance of Islamic practice. Today women in the large cities tend to play a full part in society, though they still observe the custom that prevents the free mixing of men and women.

When they go to the movies, for example, girls and women sit separately from boys and men. In rural areas, traditional attitudes are much stronger, and women usually spend most of their time in the home. It is highly unusual for a woman to drive a car. On trains, special compartments are reserved for women.

Weapons or water?
Debates between ancient and modern practices abound in both countries. For example, many people in Pakistan believe that if the country is to survive, it should develop nuclear weapons to defend itself from its powerful and often hostile neighbor India. Pakistan may already have nuclear weapons, although Pakistani leaders deny this accusation. Others believe that a poor country cannot afford to pay for such advanced technology for expensive weapons. They would prefer that the government spend more money on improving living conditions of the poor people. Running water could be brought to the villages, and there could be better health care and disease prevention. Much more money could be spent on teaching people to read and write.

In Bangladesh the debate about what the government should spend money on is more basic. Everyone agrees that growing enough food to feed all the people without foreign help is a major target. But people do not always agree on how this can be achieved. Control of annual flooding is clearly an important target if crops, as well as people's homes, are not to be lost. A program to build cyclone shelters is underway as are improvements in forecasting the arrival of cyclones. So far there are enough shelters for only a small proportion of the people in this vulnerable delta region. Flood control is very costly and requires the assistance of neighboring countries like India and Nepal. In recent years, politicians and generals have spent too much time arguing about how the country should be ruled. This has taken priority over development targets.

The "brain drain"

One of the dangers of not concentrating on reducing poverty and improving living standards is the "brain drain." Wealthier and better-educated Pakistanis and Bangladeshis take advantage of opportunities to migrate to the West. Often students sent to the United States or Europe for courses in higher education do not return. Many doctors, scientists, and engineers are lost by Pakistan and Bangladesh in this way.

In Pakistan a big problem since the independence of Bangladesh in 1971 has been the relationship between different communities. Some people even question whether there is enough in common among the Sindhis, Muhajirs, and Pushtuns to justify their staying part of the same country. Bangladesh does not have this problem because most of the people belong to the same group, the Bengalis. But the stability of Pakistan is contantly threatened by the need to keep the peace between rival ethnic communities. All these problems confront successive governments of Bangladesh and Pakistan as they strive to lead their people in the modern world without abandoning or neglecting the traditions of centuries.

Index

Afghanistan 5, 10, 17–19, 44, 72, 83
agriculture 8, 12, 14–15, 17, 19, 41–42, 54, 56, 58, 60–65, 81, 93
air travel 72, 77
architecture 14, 19, 88–89
army 28, 30–31, 33–35, 44, 48, 82, 90
arts 86
Awami League 29, 30, 34

Baluchi 44–46, 88
Baluchistan 11, 18, 24, 45, 48, 74
Bangladesh Nationalist Party 35
Bengal 18–19, 21, 24, 39, 86
Bengalis 28–29, 31–32, 41–43, 82, 94
Bhutto, Benazir 33, 35, 38, 46
Bhutto, Zulfikar Ali 33, 46
Biharis 43
boats 76–77
borders 5, 11, 14, 42, 75
British 19–21, 24, 30, 35, 41, 62, 85, 89–90

China 7, 10, 73–74
Chittagong Hill Tracts 10, 12, 39, 42, 69, 71
cities 14–15, 49–56, 74–75, 79, 82–83, 92
civil war 31
climate 11–12, 15
clothing 37, 44–45, 56
Commonwealth 35
Constitution 27–28

culture 11, 41, 85–88
cyclones 12, 59, 93–94

Dacca 11, 50, 77, 81, 89
Delhi 17–19, 21, 26
deserts 10–12
disease 79, 82–83, 93

East Pakistan 26–28, 32, 39, 43
education 46, 80–84, 93–94
energy 28, 66–67, 70–71
Ershad, General H. 35, 91
exports 28, 56, 58, 61–62, 66–69

famine 59–60, 64
fishing 14, 58, 62
flooding 8, 10, 12, 50, 59, 93–94
food 42, 51, 55–56, 58, 60–63, 79, 82–83, 93
foreign aid 28, 63–64, 93

Ganges River 8–9
government 26–28, 30, 33, 39, 42–43, 90–94

health 79–82, 93
Hindus 16, 19, 23–25, 32, 36, 39, 43, 91
housing 14, 50, 53, 54
Hyderabad 14, 46

independence 20–22, 26, 31, 32, 39, 48
India 5, 7–8, 10, 16, 18, 20–26, 30–31, 36, 39, 40–43, 46, 49, 62, 64, 72, 74, 82, 85, 93–94
Indo-Gangetic Plain 8–9, 15–16, 18
Indus River 8, 10, 15–16, 29, 46, 54

95

industry 45, 65–71
invaders 14–16, 17–19, 21, 72
Iran 5, 11, 15, 74, 91
Islam 16–17, 33–40, 56, 88, 91

Jinnah, Muhummad Ali 22–23, 26, 39

Karachi 36, 45–46, 50, 66, 75, 83
Kashmir 7, 9, 24–26, 65
Khan, General Yahya 28, 31, 33

Lahore 17, 19, 23, 50, 74, 75, 83, 89
land disputes 5, 7, 17–25
language 11, 29, 39, 41, 44, 46–48, 86, 88

medicine 79–80, 82–83, 93
Moguls 18–21, 85, 89
monsoon 12, 59–60, 78
mosques 36–38, 40, 56–57, 89
mountains 9, 10, 72–73
movies 41, 87, 92–93
Muslim League 21, 23, 39
Muslims 16–18, 21–24, 26, 32–33, 36, 38–40, 43, 48, 56–57, 91

National Assembly 28–29, 39
Nehru, Jawaharlal 22–23

parliament 28, 89, 91
partition 23–25, 26, 32, 43, 75
population 7, 8, 27, 42–43, 59–60, 63, 80
Punjab 8, 15, 17, 20, 24, 43–44, 46, 48, 83
Pushtuns 44–46, 85, 88, 94

Rahman, General Ziaur 35
Rahman, Sheikh Mujibur 29–30, 34
railroads 75, 76, 78
religion 16–17, 20, 25, 34, 36–40, 42, 89, 91
resources 65–66, 70–71
rivers 8–9, 12, 15, 61, 76–77
roads 72–75, 78

Sikhs 20, 24, 43
Sind 8, 14, 17–18, 20, 24, 45, 48
Sindhis 45–46, 88, 94
sports 66, 85, 86
Sundarbans 8, 12–13, 69

traditions 49, 94
transportation 12, 14, 50, 53, 72–77, 88, 93

United Nations 63, 83
United States 62, 85, 94

water 8, 50, 54, 60–61, 67, 71, 79, 82–83, 93
wealth 49, 51, 53, 64, 81–82, 93–94
West Pakistan 26–31, 39
wildlife 12, 13
women 36–38, 50–51, 54, 56–57, 83–84, 92–93

Zia-ul-Haq, General 33, 35, 91

© Heinemann Children's Reference 1992

This edition originally published 1992 by Heinemann Children's Reference, a division of Heinemann Educational Books, Ltd.